Praise for *Journal of a Travelling Girl*

"*Journal of a Travelling Girl* is a story filled with Tłı̨chǫ traditions, customs, beliefs, and ways of being. It is a wonderful account, told through the eyes of a young girl, of our people's ways of doing things today, guided by our strong history. The experience of travelling the Trails of Our Ancestors changes Jules, as it has many others before her, and leaves a lasting, profound impression of accomplishment, personal growth, and much hope for the future."

TAMMY STEINWAND Director, Department of Culture and Lands Protection, Tłı̨chǫ Government

"Nadine Neema honours the customs and culture of the Wekweètì community in this exquisitely told story about finding strength, healing, and acceptance. The vivid sensory details allow the reader to touch, taste, and feel the unique aspects of this journey to Behchokǫ̀. This is a must read for young readers!"

TINA ATHAIDE author of *Orange for the Sunsets*

"What a delightful read. Jules is a young girl from the south, coming of age, learning respect and responsibility, growing stronger in every way. Her relationships with the Tłı̨chǫ People, the sky, the land, the waters, and all things living and non-living give a glimpse of the gentle but insistent powers she encounters. With a foreword by a respected Elder from the community, Joseph Judas, the reader enters Jules's world feeling confident that here are lessons for all who strive to be in good relation with each other in this contemporary and complex world."

CELIA HAIG-BROWN, PHD author of *Resistance and Renewal: Surviving the Indian Residential School*

"*Journal of a Travelling Girl* is not only about people who generously welcome a young girl to share in a special journey, but it introduces readers to an important moment of history."

KATHY LOWINGER co-author (with Eldon Yellowhorn) of *What the Eagle Sees* and *Turtle Island*

In the Footsteps of the Ancestors

Journal of a Travelling Girl

Nadine Neema

Illustrations by Archie Beaverho

WANDERING FOX
An imprint of
HERITAGE HOUSE PUBLISHING

Wandering Fox Books, an imprint of
Heritage House Publishing Company Ltd.
heritagehouse.ca

*Cataloguing information available from
Library and Archives Canada*
978-1-77203-317-5 (pbk)
978-1-77203-318-2 (ebook)

Editing by Sarah Harvey and Lara Kordic,
with additional editing by Mary Metcalfe
Proofreading by Nandini Thaker
Cover and interior book design by
Setareh Ashrafologhalai
Map by Terrell Knapton-Pain

The interior of this book was produced
on 100% post-consumer paper,
processed chlorine free, and printed with
vegetable-based inks.

Heritage House gratefully acknowledges
that the land on which we live and work
is within the traditional territories of the
Lkwungen (Esquimalt and Songhees),
Malahat, Pacheedaht, Scia'new,
T'Sou-ke, and W̱SÁNEĆ (Pauquachin,
Tsartlip, Tsawout, Tseycum) Peoples.
Nadine Neema gratefully acknowledges
the land on which she works is unceded
Indigenous lands of the Kanien'kehá:ka
Nation and that Tiohtiá:ke, Montreal,
has long served as a gathering place for
diverse First Nations.

Heritage House acknowledges the
financial support of the Government
of Canada through the Canada Book
Fund (CBF) and the Canada Council
for the Arts, and the Province of British
Columbia through the British Columbia
Arts Council and the Book Publishing
Tax Credit. Nadine Neema acknowledges the financial support of the Conseil
des arts et des lettres du Québec and the
Tłı̨chǫ Government for illustrator spon-
sorship as well as ongoing guidance and
support for this special project.

24 23 22 21 20   1 2 3 4 5

Printed in Canada

To Jules, my joy and inspiration
To the People of Wekweètì, my second sèotł
And to my parents
And all of our ancestors for paving the way
May we protect the gifts you've given us
And pass them on to our children

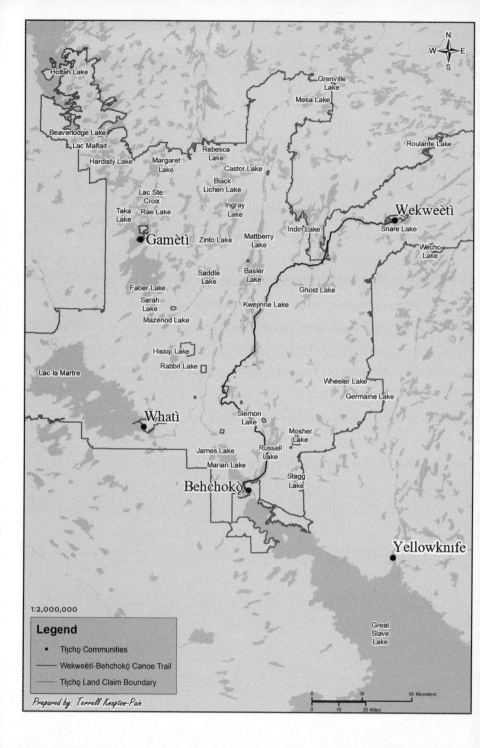

Foreword

THE COMMUNITY of Wekweètì is a very small Tłı̨chǫ community of fewer than two hundred people. We settled here in the last fifty years. Prior to that we were hunting and trapping in that area since time immemorial.

We required managers to come work in our communities to look after our corporate interests and manage our programs, to help strengthen who we are as a people. One of the managers that we hired in the late '90s was Nadine Neema. She spent a couple of years living in the community, taking part in our activities and celebrations, and coming out on the land with us. She picked up a few Tłı̨chǫ words as she got to know the Elders. She really embraced the community and learned as much as she could while she was here. We learned from her too.

We keep inviting her back and she keeps returning and sharing her skills with the community and the youth at the school through things like storytelling, music, and photography. I was the Chief of the community while Nadine was the band manager. I have known her for over twenty years. She has become like part of the community from a distance.

Nadine remains very engaged with the community after all these years. She has participated in the Tłı̨chǫ annual canoe trip, retracing the trails of our ancestors several times. Her observations from these trips come through in this story. She gives a modern look at an ancient tradition of going to the barren lands by canoe, harvesting, and engaging in our way of life.

We welcome this story. It helps document and preserve our oral history and way of life to be shared with further generations.

JOSEPH JUDAS
respected Elder and
former Chief of Wekweètì

The Departure

"I DON'T want to go!" I yelled at my mom this morning, after she told me to hurry up and get dressed.

"You say that now, but you'll see. It'll do you good." She's been saying that for weeks, and I'm sick of hearing it.

She's making me go on this canoe trip. She says I've been spending too much time moping around the house and staring at screens. But I don't feel like spending ten days disconnected from everything.

I finished getting ready and followed Mom up the road and down the long wooden steps to the dock, dragging my feet the whole way. I was cold and tired. It's the middle of summer, but I had to wear a sweatshirt and rain jacket. Thick clouds filled the sky as far as I could see. Twelve canoes lined the shores of the vast Snare Lake.

People were packing the canoes with ever-big bags of clothes, tents, and enough food to last us the trip. The whole town had come down to wish us well. About a hundred people gathered around the shore.

"This is a very important journey you'll be taking," said Mom. She put her hands on my shoulders and leaned down to look at me. She has these sparkling bluish-green eyes. I've never seen a colour quite like them. When she looks at me, it feels like she's peering into my soul. "Layla's grandparents will guide the way. Listen and watch carefully, and you'll learn a lot. You will be travelling the trails of the Tłıchǫ ancestors. The trails they've walked and paddled for thousands of years. They say if you listen carefully you might still hear them singing, *Hine'e he'e, he ho hine'e ha, hine'e he'e.*"

I didn't want to listen. I didn't want to care. I wanted to stay mad at my mom and walk away without saying goodbye. I wanted her to feel bad. I wanted to stay home watching movies, not be out here in the cold.

But I'm going to miss her. And deep down, I know she just wants what's best for me. So I hugged her tightly, burying my face in her long wavy hair and taking in her scent. Her skin is so soft. Her arms wrapped around me like a warm blanket. Then I suddenly pulled away when I felt tears coming. This will be my first time away from my mom for so long—and my first time sleeping out on the land since Uncle Joe died.

Before I continue about where we're going and why, I guess I should introduce myself. My name is Julia, but no one calls me that, except my mom when she's angry with me. Everyone else just calls me Jules.

She gave me this journal, probably to make me feel more excited about going on the trip. She knows I love keeping a record of my travels through drawing and storytelling. Even though I'm still not happy about going, I'll try writing a little every day.

I live with my mom in a tiny Tłįchǫ community in the far north of Canada called Wekweètì. The Tłįchǫ People are descendants of the Dene, an Athabaskan Indigenous People of the Northwest Territories. The community is so small and remote, you have to take a little plane from Yellowknife to get there because there's no road leading to town.

Mom and I moved there from down south when I was five. I'm eleven now. We moved because Mom got a job as the community administrator. It took a little while to get used to Wekweètì—Mom called it culture shock—but it's home now. I know almost everyone. They're like family to me. I call a lot of the grownups "Auntie" and "Uncle," even though we're not related. And I have two

best friends, Layla and Alice. They're also going on the trip, so at least I'll have good company.

After all the bags were placed in the canoes, we gathered together beside the dock where the Chief led the prayer. He has a round face, dimples, and long black silky hair. The right corner of his mouth always curls up when he talks. He prayed that we be safe on the journey, that we be guided and protected.

"I remember growing up, travelling with my parents," he said. "We were following the caribou and living in tents. Then, over the years, we settled in Wekweètì. These trails of our ancestors have existed for thousands of years. We are walking in their footsteps."

After he finished, the community stood in a line that became a circle because it was so long, and we shook everybody's hands. It's a tradition to wish the travellers a safe trip like that. I shook almost a hundred hands!

Then it was time to get in our canoes, and I was suddenly gripped with fear.

I reached for the hand of Layla's grandfather, who was right beside me. My own was trembling. "I'm scared," I admitted to him, and he helped me into the boat.

"You shouldn't be scared," he said. "Just pay attention, put on your life jacket, and be careful."

Layla's grandpa is a strong, no-nonsense man. He has dark skin and shoulder-length black-and-white hair, which is often covered by his red cap. He always wears the mukluks that Layla's grandma sewed for him, protected by black rubbers. He mostly speaks in Tłıchǫ, except when he wants to make sure we understand.

Most of the canoes have six people. But some, with kids like me, have seven. Our canoe has Layla's grandma and grandpa, her auntie, her two uncles, one of her cousins from the community of Behchokǫ̀, and me. Layla and Alice are in different canoes, so the only time we'll get to hang together is when we stop for lunch or when we set up our camps in the evenings. And during portages. That's when people walk on the trails, carrying their bags and canoes across the land, from one lake to the other.

As the canoes left the shore, people stood on the dock waving at us for a while. Mom was right at the front. My stomach felt tight as I watched her get smaller and smaller while our canoe moved farther and farther away. She couldn't come on the trip because she has too much work to do to prepare for the annual gathering happening in Behchokǫ̀, which is where we're headed.

After about an hour of paddling, we made our first stop at the Wekweètì graveyard. There are about a dozen gravesites there, each one with a rectangular picket fence a little higher than my waist. A few of them are really intricate, with little crosses or circles carved at the top of each plank. Many are painted white and blue. Some are pink or just white. Some of them look newly painted, and others look like they've been there for a long time.

Layla's great-grandpa and great-grandma are buried there. And Uncle Joe is buried there too, under a newer blue and white fence. He was the first person we really got to know when we moved to Wekweètì. He and Mom became good friends, and over the years he was like a dad to me. I never met my biological father, but I can't imagine a better one than Uncle Joe. He used to take me fishing, and he was always bringing us caribou or moose meat after hunting trips.

Uncle Joe often called me his little Tłįchǫ. Anyone can see I'm not Tłįchǫ. My skin is quite fair, and my hair is very light and curls more than any Tłįchǫ I know. But I know what he meant. I could feel it in my heart. Uncle Joe went on a lot of these canoe trips over the years. My first one was supposed to be with him. Now I don't feel like doing much of anything. I just miss him.

Alice and Layla's canoes arrived at the graveyard before ours did. They were in the gazebo waving with Layla's little cousin Kyle when I saw them. I walked over.

I met Layla and Alice in kindergarten and we have been inseparable ever since. We sat arm in arm, leaning on each other.

"I'm excited to be here," Layla said, hugging me. "Are you okay? It must be weird without your mom."

Layla is gorgeous. She has soft black hair, high cheekbones, big dark eyes, and a contagious smile. You might think someone so beautiful would be stuck up, but she's the most caring person I know. She always makes sure no one feels hurt or left out. When we first became friends, she'd come to my house regularly to ask if I could go play. When I told her I missed my grandparents, she asked hers to be mine too. Now I even call them "Grandpa" and "Grandma." I've gotten really attached. Mom's parents have come to visit a couple of times, and we've visited them a few times too. I just wish I saw them more often.

"I'm glad Mom's not here," I answered. "She's always telling me what to do, like she knows everything. I don't need her." I crossed my fingers inside my jacket pocket, hoping they couldn't tell I was terrified. I always felt safe when Uncle Joe was around. It doesn't feel right taking this trip without him.

"Yeah, parents will do that," Alice said, rolling her eyes. We all laughed. Alice is the tallest of the three of us and has the longest hair, which she usually keeps in a ponytail. She always makes me laugh. Especially in class. She gets in trouble for talking too much, but she's also very smart so it's hard for the teacher to know how to deal with her. When Alice gets moved to the front of the class, she often ends up making the quiet people talk too. I can see how frustrating that must be for the teacher, but I find it funny. When the three of us are together, she's usually the one initiating our games.

In the middle of the graveyard is the Prophet's Grave. In the centre is a tree surrounded by an unstained wooden fence the same height as the others. The pickets of the fence are thin and circular instead of rectangular like the others. Behind each of them are round rocks almost as big as soccer balls. We were standing around the grave when Layla started talking. I could tell it was an interesting story, but before she could go on everyone gathered around to pray.

The Chief talked for a while in Tłı̨chǫ. Then he began the rosary and everyone joined in. That went on for a bit, the Chief praying and everyone responding. It's so musical the way they pray.

Then everybody went quiet and bowed their heads. I'm not sure what people say in these silent prayers.

Layla started whispering. "My mother told me that years ago there was a man who helped a lot of people around here." Alice and I huddled in closer. "They say the man had visions of a rosary long before the priests

came and converted our people. They say he used to sing and his wife would dance, and that his singing made the stars dance too." She motioned to the tree at the centre of the grave. "You see how the bottom branches are tiny?"

Alice and I looked at the bottom of the tree, then we looked up to the top and back down. We both nodded.

"The top of the tree looks like a pretty Christmas tree," whispered Alice, "but the bottom looks like a small upside-down, awkward one."

"Yeah, the tree almost looks like a cross," I said, staring at it with my head tilted sideways.

"*Sshhh!*" I felt someone tapping my shoulder. It was Layla's grandma. Everyone else still had their heads down. "Prayer," she said, then bowed her head again. We put our heads down too. I wish I could hear what people are thinking in these moments. After about a minute, I looked up at Layla, really wanting to know the end of the story. She shook her head. I'd have to wait.

Finally, the prayer was over, and we all started walking towards the canoes. I was just about to ask Layla to finish her story when Alice turned to Layla's grandma.

"Can you tell us the story of how Wekweètì became a community?" she asked.

What! I thought. *What are you asking that for?* I groaned inwardly. Alice knows a lot about a lot of things. And if she doesn't know, she asks. I've learned a good deal thanks to her questions, but sometimes the answers take forever. And I was much more interested in Layla's story about why the bottom branches of the tree are so small.

Grandma smiled at Alice. "A long time ago, our people used to travel by boat and dog teams. We followed the caribou in the wintertime, and then we travelled back to Behchokǫ̀ in the spring, just like our ancestors. We would travel to the end of the lake to hunt, and when we realized the caribou were always around there, we kept coming back. That's why some of us settled in Wekweètì. And in the 1960s, we started building houses.

"It was a similar thing for the other outlying communities of Gamètì and Whatì. People discovered those were good places to fish, and so they built their houses there.

"Now, every year there is a regional Assembly in one of the four communities. Most people from the other communities fly to the Assembly, but a few hundred of us paddle. The trails we take retrace the same trails our ancestors took. In ten days, we will all meet in Behchokǫ̀ for this year's annual gathering. We will visit family and celebrate with each other. There will be a big Assembly—drum dances, feasts, hand games, and feeding the fire."

By the time Grandma had finished her story we were almost back at the boats. Layla motioned to Alice and me to come in closer. "Listen," she whispered, her eyes full of excitement. "They say that the branches of the Prophet's Tree can heal you, can make miracles happen." Her eyes opened wider, and her eyebrows went way up. She looks funny when she does that, kind of like a clown. I think she thinks it creates suspense.

She continued even more quietly. I had to strain my ears to hear. "People picked the bottom branches to be healed. Higher up where the tree widens again and the branches are full, the people couldn't reach."

"The Prophet was travelling through our community when he passed away," Alice added. "They say he was a traveller who still walks our trails."

Layla reached into her pocket and started to say something, but just then her grandpa yelled, "Come on. Let's go."

"I have to go." I hugged them both and ran to my canoe. As we paddled away from the graveyard, we saw a bald eagle's nest. There were two baby eagles inside. Grandpa said a prayer asking them to watch over us during our trip.

We've been paddling forever. Well, not me. I'm not allowed to paddle. Grandpa says I'm not ready. It would slow us down too much.

It seems like this lake is going on forever. Auntie Rosaline and Grandma look tired, but they won't let me help. It's not fair. Everybody else gets to paddle except for me. *Why did Mom send me on this trip if I have to sit here and do nothing the whole time??*

Well, it's not true that I'm doing nothing. The good part is that the water's really calm so I've been able to write and draw for the last couple of hours. It always makes me feel better when I create.

Even though everyone looks really tired, they keep laughing like little children. I wish I felt their excitement. They're talking about celebrations and drum dances in Behchokǫ̀. Grandma says this year the Assembly is more special than other years. Something about land claims and self-government. Boring stuff.

The Secret Branch

WE FINALLY arrived at our campsite in the early evening. There's a large clearing very close to the water where people carried their bags and started setting up tents. The land is soft and spongy. The clearing is like a huge oval, so we can see all the tents at once.

"Ever beautiful island!" Alice exclaimed.

"There are blueberries everywhere!" Layla added.

"Did you know there are infinite shades of green?" Alice said dreamily, looking up at the trees.

I looked around. The greens all looked the same to me. I was thinking of Uncle Joe. The last time I camped on the land was with him. Since he died, the sound of

his voice has been fading from my mind, almost as if he was just a dream.

Layla pulled me into a small space between the trees and Alice followed. It was just big enough for the three of us to talk privately. Layla held both my hands and looked very serious. I knew she had something important to say.

"We took this from the bottom of the Prophet's Tree," she whispered and pulled something out of her jacket pocket. It was a tiny branch about the size of a rabbit's foot. She gave it to Alice, who handed it to me, creating a kind of ritual. "We want you to have it."

"What for?" I said, feeling those tears rising up again.

"So it can heal you," Alice answered.

"How?"

"I'm not sure how it works." Layla thought for a bit, then looked at me softly. "Maybe you need to rub it where it's hurting."

"Okay, thanks," I said, and hugged them both. I have no idea what I'll do with the branch because it hurts everywhere. Besides, I don't really believe in that stuff. But I'm grateful to have such good friends. I put it in my pocket, and we set off to explore the campsite. We ran around watching the different camps take shape—fires being made, tents coming up, clothes being hung. It was cool watching a little community emerge out of nothing.

Back at my camp, Grandma was making tea and cooking bannock and caribou ribs. Alice, Layla, her cousin Kyle, and I went to pick blueberries with Auntie Rosaline. Well, Kyle spent more time pretending to shoot imaginary caribou, but the rest of us picked a lot of blueberries.

Auntie Rosaline is a quiet, wise woman. She doesn't say much but teaches a lot through her actions. She always has her hair braided and sometimes does mine too.

I love this time of year because of the midnight sun. It doesn't get dark, so we stay up late playing outside. Whenever Kyle is with us, he follows me everywhere. It doesn't bother me so much, except when we're playing hide and seek because he can't hide silently. He's almost five, and I love how innocent his mind is. But he often has snot coming out of his nose that he wipes on his arm.

I'M LYING in my sleeping bag. I can't sleep. I'm sharing a big tent with Grandma and Grandpa, who are already snoring away. My feet are cold.

I pull the little branch from my pocket. I look at it carefully. It's soft if I rub it downwards, and it smells nice. I try to think about where it's hurting. I rub it on my heart. I do it for a while in case it might help me heal from missing Uncle Joe. It feels funny, but I continue anyway.

DAY 2

No Fun
at All

THIS MORNING was ever peaceful. I woke up still holding the branch against my heart. The sky was so clear that a few people said it was the perfect day for paddling. We ate blueberry pancakes that Auntie Rosaline made. She makes the best pancakes. Then we packed our tents, picked up all the garbage and burned it. After that, everyone from the twelve canoes gathered behind Grandpa at the edge of the lake. He prayed for our safe travel to the next camp by making an offering of berries from our breakfast. Then we were off, under the sunny blue sky.

We hadn't been travelling for very long when the sky turned completely dark. A massive storm came out of nowhere! Everyone paddled really hard to get to shore. The water was rough and kept coming into the boat. I was scared we would tip. I started to cry.

"Stay calm," Grandpa said, as he paddled swiftly and steadily. "Keep your body low. Worrying won't do anything."

When we got to shore, we covered our canoe with a big tarp and crouched under it, waiting for the storm to pass. The rain came down hard on my back, and the thunder was really loud. My heart was racing. I wished Mom had come. Grandpa told me to sit still and wait, so I held Grandma's hand until it was over. Finally, the rain stopped, and the sun returned. We removed the tarp, and the perfect day was back! We set off paddling again in the calm water.

The lake went on forever, and again I had nothing to do. My urge to paddle returned even stronger than before. So I pleaded with Auntie to let me try. She gave me her paddle and quickly showed me how to dip it into the water with solid, even strokes. I had paddled a couple of times with Uncle Joe, but that paddle was smaller and we travelled at a much slower pace. Most of the time we were in a motorboat. This paddle was heavier than I thought, and I couldn't keep up with the speed that everyone was going. The paddle slipped out of my hands and into the water. We had to turn the canoe around to get it. Grandpa was *not* happy.

"When the time is right, I will show you," he said firmly. "Right now, we need to keep going, and you are not ready. Everything has its time. Yours will come."

I felt bad for letting everyone down, but Grandpa made me feel worse. I wanted to yell at him at the top of my lungs: *It's so boring sitting in the canoe doing nothing while everyone else gets to paddle! I want to go home! I don't care about travelling the paths of the ancestors! They aren't even* my *ancestors!*

Grandma looked at me with her big smile and kind, gentle eyes. Her long salt-and-pepper hair was tied back in a ponytail. She put her hand on my cheek and said, "Be patient, my girl. Look at the land. It's better than television. Look at the life around you. Enjoy the view."

So that's what I did. And just before reaching our new camp, we saw two moose swimming across the lake. They were so big and right in front of us! They looked majestic with their gigantic antlers shooting up above the water. It was like a nature movie. We saw lots of loons too. I love that they have so many different songs.

I could hear little Kyle imitating their calls from his canoe.

The new campsite is cool. We have to walk up a long trail through the trees to get to the opening in the forest. All the tents and campfires are in different places and more spread out than yesterday. I had to climb over rocks and run around trees before I found Alice and Layla. When we finally found each other, we pretended to be explorers looking for hidden treasures.

We searched by the edge of the forest, crouching near the ground. "Look what I found!" Alice yelled over to us. She was holding a piece of birch bark twice the size of her hand. We gathered around her. "Look here," she said, pointing at a straight line of little holes all along the top edge. "These holes are obviously manmade, but what do you think they're for?"

"I have no idea!" Layla answered, inspecting it carefully. We found her mother, who told us it must have been from a canoe or a basket made a long time ago.

"Wow. It really feels like our ancestors have travelled here before," Layla said, raising her eyebrows.

Alice declared it was time to play hide and seek. We ran around playing for a while, but Kyle kept following me and giving me away. I was always trying to run from

him. Just as I was ducking behind a big rock, Grandpa spotted me.

"Hey, what are you girls doing over there?" he scolded. "You think you don't have to help?"

Layla, Alice, and I all emerged sheepishly from our hiding spots as Grandpa began his lecture.

"In the old days, when I was your age, before we built houses in Wekweètì, we lived in tents. When we ran out of supplies, some of the men had to go back to Behchokǫ̀ by dog team. While they were out getting supplies we waited in the community in our tents. In the middle of winter it was very cold, and the four corners of the tent were covered in snow. We would all gather in the centre around the fire. But to keep the fire going, the women and older children would have to go out in the bush and collect wood. If we didn't have snowshoes, it was difficult because the snow was deep, so we would make sure to get lots of wood when we went out. When we returned to the tent, all the kids would come out and help chop the wood and prepare for the next day."

From now on, he said, he expected us to help. "First thing we do when we get somewhere is to collect wood, make a fire, and set up camp. When all that is done and no one needs help cooking or doing something, *then* you can go play."

I felt my blood boiling. *I spend the whole day bored in the canoe, and now that I'm finally with my friends I have to work?* I wanted to yell. *This trip is no fun at all!*

But what else could I do? Layla and Alice returned to their camps, and I reluctantly started cleaning up. I dried the dishes after Auntie washed them. Then we wrapped them in dishtowels and put them away. I helped put the food away too. When we were done, I went off to find Alice and Layla.

We pretended to be explorers again. We ran around to all the different camps. Some people were playing cards, some were telling stories or jokes around a fire. Clothes and shoes were hanging on ropes tied between trees. Tea was brewing at every camp.

As we ran through the trees, Alice hit her head on one of the hanging shoes. "Ouch!"

"You okay?" Layla and I both said, turning around and banging into each other.

"Owww!" We both fell down.

"Are *you* okay?" Alice asked. We all started laughing. We laughed for a while. I couldn't stop, which made Alice and Layla laugh even more. It turned into a crazy laughing fit. I can't remember the last time I laughed so much.

We kept exploring. We saw Uncle Jimmy, Auntie Rosaline, Alice's older brother, and others playing poker. We watched them for a while. Uncle Jimmy has short black hair and a missing tooth on the bottom front. He laughs with a deep chuckle that sounds so joyful. He's also a good bluffer. I saw him double down even though he didn't have a pair, and half the table folded. I wish I could play too, but they play for real money. It isn't for kids.

Later, we went back to my camp and sat around the fire next to Grandma. We listened to Grandpa talk about Chief Monfwi, one of the greatest Tłįchǫ chiefs of all time. Once he started a story, he could talk all night.

"Every summer, some of us Tłįchǫ travel the trails of our ancestors, the same trails Chief Monfwi and our ancestors walked for thousands of years," he said. "In the old days, we travelled with dog teams. When we were travelling, our parents knew the good spots for fishing and hunting, and we would camp there because that's how we ate. It was really hard in those days. We had to get enough fish to feed the dogs too. Under their paws they would get sores. We would make them little mittens out of caribou hide if they cut themselves on rocks."

I was starting to feel sleepy. Grandpa continued, "Some days, if we didn't get enough fish, we couldn't

feed the dogs enough. If this happened too often, we would stay in the same place for a couple of nights to catch more fish and make sure the dogs ate and got stronger. Sometimes, when there were caribou up ahead, the dogs would notice even before we did. They would forget about their paws hurting, and they would start running fast to catch up to the caribou."

I lay down with my head on Grandma's lap and watched the fire.

Grandpa started talking about how the annual gathering this year would be different. "We will finally have our own government and become owners of our land," he said. I think I drifted off to sleep, because I don't remember what came next. I dreamt I was walking the trails with my ancestors. We were singing and dancing, and we could fly.

Then I heard Uncle Jimmy laughing and I opened my eyes. I still had that glorious feeling of being able to fly. I left everyone by the fire and came back to our tent to write about the day. I'm done now and ready to fall back asleep. Goodnight.

DAY 3

Working Together

I HEARD today would be the first day of portages, so I was very excited to get going. I wouldn't have to sit in the canoe all day. We packed up and gathered around Grandpa, who led our morning prayer. He asked the Creator for our safe journey to the next camp and for the Spirit of our ancestors to guide us.

At the start of one of the portages, we saw a bird's nest that was so perfect it looked like a precious piece of art that someone had made for Easter. Inside, there were eight or nine eggs placed in two circles. It was just sitting there by itself in the long swampy grass. Grandma told us they were duck eggs. I couldn't believe that was made by a duck.

The trails went on forever. I lost my sweater on one of them, and Uncle Gordie had to go back with me to look for it. Uncle Gordie's very strong. He looks like he could carry anything. I always see him working when I pass his house, building a new shed or fixing a vehicle, and never without his blue cap. He doesn't speak much English, but we always manage to understand each other. He looks out for me a lot.

We searched for my sweater for a while before we finally found it on a rock where I had stopped with the girls for a break. Grandpa was ever mad.

"You have to look after your own things," he scolded. "We are only passing through. We will not be coming back on our tracks, and we do not have time to search for things left behind. We still have a long way to travel to Behchokǫ̀. You are careless, and that can be dangerous. Pay attention."

I hate how Grandpa is so strict with me, but Grandma explained it's his way of teaching me.

"In the old days, this was our way of life," she said softly. "We were always travelling, and if we forgot things along the way we could find ourselves in serious trouble. Our boats were made of canvas. We would paint them. Sometimes when we went over rocks, we would get a hole in the boat. We had to go to land and get spruce gum from the trees to patch up the holes. We always kept extra gum with us because we knew we would need it. If we forgot to carry the spruce gum with us and got a big hole in the middle of a lake, it could cause our boat to sink."

Grandma is so patient when she explains things to me. She makes me feel better. She amazes me. She is old, has pain in her knees, and walks with a hunched back, but she always works very hard. She carries her own bag on the trails, helps chop wood at night, and always cooks dinner.

We walked *so* much today. Some of the trails went on for hours. We walked and walked and walked. Then lots of people walked back to the beginning of the trail to get the rest of the stuff. Uncle Gordie carried a huge canvas bag with the strap against his forehead and another huge bag on top. I saw several men doing that. I don't know how they do it.

All the bags and all the boats had to be carried across. I carried my knapsack and the life jackets. I could hardly carry my own body by the end. It's really hard work. By the time we got to the campsite, I thought my feet would fall off.

I helped set up our camp. Uncle Gordie and Grandpa cut wood for the fire, and I helped gather kindling. That's what smaller pieces of starter wood are called. I searched for the driest pieces because those burn the best. Afterward, I saw Uncle Jimmy and Auntie Rosaline tying a rope between two trees so we could dry our wet clothes. I helped them hang stuff. Our clothes and shoes are always getting wet, from a storm or a swampy portage or water in the canoe. It's impossible to stay dry! After that, I watched them set up our tent and helped put our things inside.

Grandma showed me how to pick *orì* to sit on. "Go to an orì tree and break the branch off like this." She cut

branches off a spruce tree. "Then you can weave them together to sit on."

The men made a tipi with a fire in the middle. We connected one orì branch to another and another so they were interlocking, until we had made a carpet big enough for everyone to sit on. We gathered around the fire to eat. It felt good to help set up our camp.

"I remember Chief Jimmy Bruneau's wife," Grandpa said. "She was such a hard worker. She would wake up at 5:00 a.m., make the fire, get a pan full of snow, and put it on the open fire. If there was black soot in the pan, she would drain it through the spruce bowl, and clear water would go in the basin. Then she would take the basin with clean water around to the people and tell them to wash their faces and hands before the day started.

"Seeing everyone work hard tonight, helping each other set up the camp, reminded me of Jimmy Bruneau's wife," he said.

"Who's Chief Bruneau?" I asked.

"Jimmy Bruneau became Chief after Chief Monfwi passed away. His vision was that our children would be educated without losing our language and culture, that they would be taught both ways, our way and the white man's way."

After dinner, I helped Auntie wash the dishes with the lake water. Then I went to find my friends. Like on the first night, this campsite is tiny, so all the tents are very close together. I found the girls and Kyle right away.

"Look at the moon!" Kyle said excitedly. "I want to touch it. I think it's moving. Do you think it might come down to us?"

"No," I told him. "The moon always stays in the sky."

"I think it's trying to come to us," he answered. "I think it wants to be our friend and play with us."

We walked around for a while. "How are you feeling?" Layla asked me, intertwining her arm in mine. Then her voice dropped to a whisper. "Is the branch helping?"

"I'm not sure yet." I wanted to say more, but I didn't know what to say. I'd completely forgotten I had the branch, but I didn't want her to know that.

"I'm sure it will help you," Alice said. "It's helped ever lots of people."

We were too tired to play for long, so we came back to my camp and sat next to Grandpa by the fire. People were gathered around listening to him talk about Chief Monfwi.

"A long time ago, Chief Monfwi signed a treaty for the Tłı̨chǫ," Grandpa said. "It was called Treaty 11. Back then, we used to travel on the land, following the caribou during the winter months. We fed our families, made dry meat, and tanned the hides. In the summer, we would return to Behchokǫ̀ to trade furs and fish.

"When the white man began to govern the North, our land and way of life became threatened. Chief Monfwi signed the treaty and said, 'As long as the sun rises, the river flows, and the land does not move, we will not be restricted from our way of life.'"

"What exactly is a treaty?" Alice asked Grandma.

"It's an agreement between us and the government of Canada. Treaty 11 was meant to protect our language, culture, and way of life," she answered.

"So the treaty was a good thing for us?" Alice asked.

"Well, it was supposed to be. It opened the door for us and the government to talk, but it took a long time for us to understand each other. And over time, issues arose."

"What kind of issues?" Alice probed.

"We and the government understood the treaty to mean different things," Grandma explained patiently, "especially the parts about our rights and the use of our traditional land."

I didn't really understand, but I figured it was one of those times when I should just keep quiet and listen.

Mom always tells me to listen well when the Elders are talking, that I will learn more from them than from any book, even more than I would learn from her. Besides, Alice and Layla were very absorbed, so I nodded my head too. I have a feeling we'll be hearing a lot more about this on the trip.

~~~~~~~

I'M CURLED up in my sleeping bag, holding the branch to my nose so I can take in its delicious fragrance. I put it down next to my face and slowly fall asleep.

DAY 4

Hand Games

I'M AFRAID to go to sleep. I'm terrified the Big Animal will come into my tent tonight. We never say his name because that can call him to us. His claws are huge and so are his teeth.

The day started out fine. We packed our bags, said our prayers, and paddled away. We had another really long portage, but I didn't get as exhausted this time. Then the wind became very strong, and the water was rough and choppy. Everyone paddled very hard. I was scared the water would come in the boat again, but I stayed low and didn't say anything.

We stopped for lunch on the shores of a big island. After we ate, people asked if they could throw their leftover bones in the fire. The Chief said yes because we wouldn't be sleeping here. We never put bones in the fire in a place where we'll be setting up camp because the smell could attract the Big Animal. But in the end, the water was too rough to paddle through safely, and the Chief decided we *would* be sleeping here after all.

I'll try to write more about all the good things that happened today so that I can forget that I'm scared. Like Grandpa says, there's no use in worrying.

After lunch, we had a great time exploring the island. The entire place is covered in a grey, mossy carpet. It's so soft on my feet. A bunch of us went swimming. We played in the water and washed our hair. We jumped off rocks into the lake and compared who could make the biggest splash.

Then we ran around the island on the soft cushion of moss. Little Kyle noticed that the moon was already in the sky. "Look at the moon!" he said. "Why are the moon and the sun in the sky at the same time?"

Auntie Rosaline answered, "The moon and the sun are secretly in love. They are very shy, and in order not to show their love, one appears during the day and the other during the night. But sometimes they cannot resist, and they need to look at each other's faces, so they both come out together."

"Oh!" said Kyle. "I love them too."

After supper, the men played hand games. I love watching them. Two teams sit in a line, facing each other. The men on one team do a kind of dance with their hands, each man showing a little object he's holding. Others play drums and sing behind them. Then the men put their hands under their coats so they can

hide the object in one of their two hands without the other team seeing which one. They pull their dancing arms out, and someone from the other team tries to guess which hand the object is in while doing his own cool hand gestures. If they guess the correct hand, that person is out, and he joins the drummers. I'm not sure exactly how it ends, but there's a lot of cheering and exchanging of sticks when a team wins.

"My dad told me that our ancestors used to play hand games as a way of gambling for things they needed," Layla said.

"What kind of things?" I asked.

"Furs, matches, toboggans, dogs. Whatever they needed," Alice answered.

The men taught Kyle the rules of hand games, and he played a little with them. He was really excited to be part of it. It was ever cute. As the men sang, I felt like I could hear the ancestors singing too.

Afterwards, I went back to my camp to sit around the fire. Grandpa was talking about the Treaty again and how it wasn't properly respecting their rights and traditional use of the land.

"Our way of life was being threatened," he said. "So we formed a Dogrib Council to represent the four communities and negotiate a proper agreement for our people. This agreement is called the Tłįchǫ Agreement. It recognizes our rights and brings alive the words of Chief Monfwi."

I asked Grandma why sometimes they were called Dogrib and sometimes Tłįchǫ. She answered, "Dogrib is the English word for Tłįchǫ. We began using it when we started speaking English with the white man. In our language we are called Tłįchǫ, and we are a tribe of the Dene People."

I really like hearing stories of how things used to be. I'm starting to look forward to ending the day that way. Even though it isn't my culture, Grandma, Grandpa, and the others have always made me feel like family. I'm going to miss these nightly stories when the trip is over.

Okay. I tried writing about the day to feel better. But I'm still scared. I'm still thinking about the bear.

Oh no! I just said his name!

I REMEMBER the branch. I grab it from my pocket and start rubbing it in my hand. My heart is racing. I feel sick to my stomach with fear. I want to run back to the fire, but I'm too scared to move.

I begin to pray. I've never prayed on my own before. I'm not sure how to start. "Dear branch," I say. That sounds weird. "Dear Uncle Joe." That's better, but I should include the Creator.

"Dear Creator, Uncle Joe, branch, and all the ancestors watching over us. Please don't let the Big Animal come into our camp tonight. Please keep us safe. I miss you, Uncle Joe. Goodnight."

I feel a little better, but I still can't sleep. My breathing is heavy. I think about the songs of the ancestors. I rub the branch on my chest. That's where it hurts. I want to sing one of those songs to help protect me, but I don't know how it goes.

The Abandoned Cabin

I'M SO tired, almost too tired to write. Today was the hardest day of the trip so far.

During one of the portages, I fell through the deep wet moss. I wasn't paying attention, and my foot went right through to a yucky bed of muddy water. I was all wet and gross. Water went up my leg and in my boots.

And the mosquitoes were killing me. They've been bad all week, but this was the worst. I thought I'd get eaten alive. I could feel them taking chunks out of my skin. I was itchy everywhere. I could hardly breathe without one going in my mouth or up my nose. The loud buzzing was driving me crazy.

We did three or four portages. Two of them took at least three hours each. During one portage I asked what time it was, and Uncle Jimmy told me two o'clock. When I asked again at the end of that portage, it was already five.

We didn't even stop for lunch. We had snacks in the canoe and then portaged the rest of the time. I carried our tent, life jackets, and paddles. It was long, it was hard, and it was heavy. And there were bugs everywhere. We portaged up and down the mountains. Sometimes the land was soft and spongy, and other times it was all rock.

Between the two longest portages, there was no clean water to drink. The lake that separated them was small and swampy, and we couldn't drink from it. We had to fill up our water bottles before the first portage and make them last until the end of the second one. I ran out of water partway through. When we reached that next lake, I was so happy to finally drink again. I drank and drank. And then I had the hiccups so I had to drink some more.

During one of the portages, the ground was too wet and too swampy to walk across. Uncle Gordie and other men cut down some trees to make us a bridge. I thought I'd be really scared to walk on the bridge, but I wasn't. I thought of the branch in my pocket, and I walked across easily. I even went back to get more things. Kyle sat at the end of the trail, leaning against one of the canvas bags and smiling to himself, too tired to even play.

Suddenly a gunshot rang out! It was so loud I thought I'd popped an eardrum. Grandma told us to stay put until we knew it was safe to go on. For a few minutes, we didn't know what was going on, but then Uncle Jimmy appeared in front us, from the direction of the shot.

"We spotted the Big Animal up ahead," he said.

My heart skipped a beat and I squealed, "What?"

He looked at me and smiled with his missing tooth. "Don't worry, Jules. Gordie fired a shot into the sky, and the bear left. The coast is clear now. Just make sure to stick together!"

I was a little shaken up when we started walking again, but when the sun came out I almost forgot about the hulking beast—especially when we arrived at our campsite this evening and saw an old abandoned cabin. It was unlike anything I've seen on this trip and looked totally out of place.

"Who built this?" I wondered out loud.

"That was a prospector's cabin," Grandma told me.

"What's a prospector?" I asked.

"A prospector is a type of explorer who looks for minerals," she said.

"They were probably looking for gold," Alice added.

Layla, Alice, and I went inside the cabin together. Kyle followed.

"Ever cool!" Alice looked around curiously.

The cabin was an abandoned mess. There was a rusty old bathtub and tattered curtain, a rickety-looking bed with a lumpy mattress that probably had stuff living in it, and a broken plastic chair. There was a wooden table that looked pretty clean except for the moulding papers and a large book sitting on top.

"Why does it look like whoever was here left in a hurry?" I asked.

"I'm not sure, but I'd say that's how things were done," Alice answered. "The Elders have often talked about the mess that old miners left behind, how they never cleaned up after themselves." She picked up the big book and began flipping through it carefully. "I wonder what this book is about."

"It probably holds the secrets of this place," Layla said. Her eyes widened and her eyebrows rose.

"What kind of secrets?" Kyle asked excitedly.

"Never mind," she said and smiled. "You're too young to understand." I didn't know what she meant either, but I didn't say anything.

"It looks like some kind of field guide the prospector was using," Alice explained, examining its pages.

There was also a shelf with Magic Baking Powder, salt, pepper, sugar, and other spices, a kettle, and a frying pan. And a battered old outdoor toilet too. We ran around exploring. After we were done, we played tug of war on the giant sandy beach. A bunch of us fell into the water when the other side let go of the rope.

I went back to my camp to change into dry clothes, and when I came out of the tent I saw Grandpa and Uncle Jimmy fishing. Watching them reminded me of Uncle Joe. I learned everything I know about fishing from him. I went to join them.

I caught an ever-big trout that Grandpa helped me reel in. He and Uncle Jimmy caught some too, and Auntie Rosaline and Grandma prepared them. They scaled the fish and took out all the bones and made filets. We shared the fish with other camps. Grandma also showed me how to make bannock. What a delicious supper!

I didn't go sit by the fire tonight. I barely have the energy to write. I'm too tired. I have to go to sleep.

❦

I STRETCH out on my mattress. It feels good to lie down. I hold the little branch against my heavy head. I rub it back and forth gently and fall asleep like that. I wake up with it still pressed against my cheek.

The Old Grave

IT WAS another huge day of portages with ever lots of rapids. During one of them, two people stayed in each canoe and paddled through the rapids while the rest of us walked. I love those kinds of portages. We don't have to carry anything. We walk across while our things stay in the canoe.

We watched the boats arrive safely at the other end. It looked like so much fun. I told Grandma they should always take the rapids during every portage. She said it takes a lot of skill to paddle through the rapids, and it can be very dangerous.

On one of the portages I got into a lot of trouble. It was an ever-long trail, and partway through there was a gigantic waterfall. A bunch of us went to look at it.

"Ever nice!" Alice squealed with excitement.

"It's amazing!" I agreed, mesmerized. "I've never seen such a huge waterfall before." The gushing water was so powerful.

We stood and stared for a while. I wanted to stay all day. Then Auntie Rosaline said it was time to go. We headed back to the trail. After a while, I realized I'd forgotten my bag. I didn't want to say anything and be told I was careless, so I just went back quickly without telling anyone. I thought, *If I run, I'll be back before they know it.*

I ran to the falls to find the bag. It was on the ground exactly where I thought it would be. I picked it up and almost rushed off. But the water was pouring down, crashing into the river with so much force. The roaring sound calmed me. I closed my eyes for a moment. I loved how the moisture in the air felt on my face. And I loved watching the water rushing around the rocks.

I finally left and started running down the trail. The shrubs kept getting bigger and bigger, until I realized I

wasn't on the trail anymore. I turned back but couldn't find the path. I was lost. I searched for a while. I was alone for a long time. I was scared.

I reached into my pocket and held the little branch tightly. "Dear Creator, dear Uncle Joe, dear Tree, dear all the ancestors on this trail. Please help me find my way back. I promise I'll be more careful. I'll always listen, and I won't wander off alone anymore. If you could help me just this once, please, I'll pay attention from now on."

Just then, I heard Auntie Rosaline and Uncle Jimmy calling my name. I took a deep breath. "I'm here!" I yelled. I squeezed the branch, looked up, and said, "Thank you!"

Auntie hugged me tightly. "Don't you ever do that again!" she exclaimed. She sounded so happy to see me but also very angry. I tried to explain that I had forgotten my bag, but I knew it didn't matter.

When we got to the boats, Grandpa was furious. "You have no idea the danger you put yourself in. Never walk these trails alone. Always walk in groups. And never go anywhere without letting an adult know."

I knew he was right. "I'm sorry," I said with my head down. "I won't do it again." And I meant it.

The campsite tonight is enormous. From one end of "town," where the first crew put their tents, to the other end seems like a mile. There's so much space between tents and camps. I love how our village keeps changing each night.

There's an old grave by the water. It has a similar picket fence to the ones at the Wekweètì cemetery, but the wood is a lot older. And the pickets are round like the ones at the Prophet's Grave. We all gathered around, and Grandpa prayed to the Creator to be with the man buried there and to protect us on our journey.

After the prayer, I turned to Alice and said, "It's kind of creepy to see an old grave along these trails, don't you think?"

"They say because the man died here, his spirit still lingers," she answered. "And if you pray to him when you pass through, he will protect you on the trail."

"I wonder what his story is. How did he die?" I asked.

"Who knows?" Layla responded with her eyes full of intrigue. "There are so many legends on these trails."

I thought of Uncle Joe. I wondered if his spirit lingered somewhere too. I've been praying to him, but I don't know if he hears me. I don't know if anyone hears me.

I helped gather kindling to make the fire. I walked around with Uncle Gordie, looking for small dry pieces. Then I helped set up our tent.

First I clicked the poles into place, then Uncle Gordie slipped them into the fabric. I gave him the pegs, and he anchored the tent to the ground. He showed me how to push the pegs in with the heel of my foot.

Grandpa looked at me and smiled.

"I love setting up our home in a different place each night," I told him. I put our sleeping bags in the tent and went to find the others.

Kyle ran over when he saw me. "Look at all the stars," he said, staring at the sky. There were ever lots of stars out. "I think they are all babies of the moon. The moon is the mommy. She will protect us while we sleep." What he said was very cute but also meaningful to him. I realized each of us make our own meanings. We each find whatever it is that makes us feel safe.

We played Bubble Gum. "Bubble gum, bubble gum in the dish. How many bubble gums do you wish?" Alice sang as she tapped all of our fists. The last person was me.

"Seven!" I said. Alice counted to seven and it fell on Kyle so he was out. He was upset to be the first one out, so Layla suggested we let him play again. We played for a while, then we went to eat. I helped Uncle Gordie fetch water from the lake.

Later, Grandpa sat on a rock and told the four of us stories about life in the old days.

"Life is easy now," he said. "Whatever you need, you can get easily. Back then it wasn't like that. It was hard to get things. We couldn't just go to the store whenever we wanted. We had to make our own caribou jackets and pants. We used the caribou hide from August because we knew it was thick and would keep us warm. We wore the fur on the inside so we wouldn't get cold."

I sat quietly, listening carefully, interested in every detail. I didn't fidget or get bored once.

"Before we got power and fuel to heat the place, all we had was candles and lanterns. We made our own wood stoves with forty-five-gallon barrels. If we ran out of candles, we had to make our own with caribou fat. To get water in winter, we had to make a hole through the ice with a chisel. It was hard to get food too. We had to catch all our food. We caught rabbits, fish, muskrat, caribou . . ." He named a whole bunch of animals. "Now we have store-bought meat and canned foods. Now you can just put a mattress down and go to sleep. Back then, you needed to have caribou hide."

Their world has changed so much so fast, I thought. *Mom says the whole world has.*

"Seeing the grave today reminded me of how things used to be," he went on. "It's important to know where you come from to appreciate what you have. And like Chief Bruneau said, 'to be strong like two people.'"

I want to be strong like two people too.

The Dream

I JUST woke up. Everyone else is still sleeping. The sun is coming up over the horizon, and the mist is crawling across the lake.

I dreamt I was lying in my tent and the spirit of an Elder came to me. He sat at the end of my mattress. At first I was petrified. I didn't know what it was. He told me not to be afraid. His voice was ever loving.

Then he spoke in a more serious but still loving tone. "You must be vigilant on the trails, my child. Your actions can put you in severe danger. They can cost you your life. And they can put other people in danger too. You must pay attention and be careful. You cannot be lazy. Look after yourself. Look after each other. Travel safely

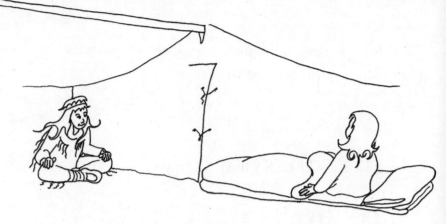

and together. This is how you survive on the land. And when you have done everything you can to be prepared, remember you are still at the mercy of the elements around you. Then, all you can do is surrender to the Great Spirit."

And then he disappeared. It was a dream, but it was ever real. I tried to draw what he looked like so I won't forget.

I feel it was the spirit of the man buried on this island. I feel that somehow he's still here. Maybe the ancestors really do keep watching over us when they pass. Maybe Uncle Joe does hear me when I talk to him.

Everyone is still asleep. The birds are chirping, and the wolves are howling in the distance. There's a little village of people snoring. It reminds me how small we all are in this great big world.

I LAY my head down on the tiny branch. There are hardly any needles left. Most of them have been rubbed off. But it still gives me comfort.

DAY 7, LATER

Our Tipi

TODAY I paddled! Grandpa said I was ready, and he let me try. It was ever great! It took a lot of concentration and coordination. My strokes had to be very consistent so I could keep up with the rhythm of everyone else. I felt a bit tired after a while, but I didn't want to stop. I *loved* it! I loved the feeling of being part of the team, of pushing the water back, knowing that the boat was moving forward because of me. I felt so much purpose.

Uncle Jimmy was sitting behind me, and a few times I splashed him by accident when I lifted the paddle out of the water. At least it was a warm day so it wasn't so bad. And he didn't seem to mind.

We paddled all day. Well, I didn't paddle all day, but I did paddle for a long time. We made little stops along the way to wait for the other canoes. We saw an eagle flying above us and a moose standing at the edge of the woods near the water. It looked so grand. We also saw a family of loons. Grandpa told a story about how these animals used to be human.

"They wanted to become animals, so they were given wings and became what we call the loon. The raven saw them diving in the water and coming up and plunging back in again. He saw they were happy and enjoying themselves, and he was jealous. He wanted to do that too. He asked to become like them, but he was told he needed to talk like them to become like them. He tried to make their sound, but instead he cawed like a crow. So, he had to keep being a raven. He was angry and threw mud on the loons. That's why today they have that grey spot on their heads."

At one point it got very windy, and we stopped for lunch in a big clearing in the forest near the water. Some of the younger men put lots of wood in a pile and made a big fire.

The wind was blowing ever strong. The fire became huge. At first it looked cool. Then people came running

to help put it out, and I realized it was out of control. "Get water. *Hurry!*" I heard someone yell. There was a lot of commotion. For a moment I thought the whole camp might burn down.

It made me think about my dream, about what the spirit had said: we need to look after each other and be careful. We could have burned down the forest today. We could have gotten really hurt. Anything can happen when we don't pay attention. I resolved to be mindful.

The camp tonight is tiny. It's on the thin point of an island. When we first arrived, each side of the point had a very distinct view from the other—there seemed to be two lakeshores, two completely different skies with contrasting clouds, and very different light. It was almost as if I could see two separate worlds by just turning my head.

The loons were singing their sweet songs. And the sun took forever to set. It was pink and white, then orange. The mist was rising over the lake. It was like a painting.

"Wow! Look at the bubble around the moon," Kyle exclaimed. There was a bright ring of light around the moon. "Why is it there?" he asked.

"I guess it's the moon's light making that bubble," I answered.

Kyle appeared to consider that for a moment. "I think it's the sun that is sleeping next to the moon," he said. "I think the sun loves the moon so he wants to sleep next to her. And that's the sun's light shining around the moon."

"I think you're right," I said with a smile.

Alice, Layla, and I built a little tipi. We gathered a lot of tree branches and connected them together. When we got stuck, we asked Uncle Gordie and Alice's dad to help us. They cut some longer tree branches and connected them all on top. It made a tipi almost twice as high as me, with an opening in front. In that opening, about halfway up, we put smaller branches across, leaving space for the door below.

"It's like our own little home in this great new town!" Alice said.

We played there for a long time. Auntie Rosaline, Grandma, and Alice's mom came to visit. They helped us pick spruce branches to make an orì carpet so we could all sit comfortably.

"Would you like some tea?" I asked, pretending to hold a teapot.

"Oh sure," Grandma said and extended her imaginary cup.

"With milk and one sugar," Auntie added. Everyone laughed.

We had the best tea party. Then the adults helped us collect some wood to make a mini fire outside. Grandma told me how well I had paddled.

"I am proud of you, my girl," she said. "You have grown so much on this journey. You are taking your place on these trails and in this world."

She fed the fire with some tobacco and said a prayer for our continued safety and growth on this trip. The three of them left shortly after that, but Alice, Layla, and I hung out in the tipi for most of the night. We talked about places where our bodies were aching from the trip. We showed each other our blisters, scratches, and mosquito bites.

"I'm the winner!" I said. "I have the most scars from this trip."

"Lucky you!" Alice replied. We started laughing. We laughed a lot about silly things. Then Layla got more serious.

"This is going to be our last year of school in Wekweètì," she said. "Where do you think you'll go to high school?"

"Behchokǫ̀ or Yellowknife," answered Alice. "I'm not sure yet."

"I guess it depends where my mom will be working," I said. I felt a pang in my heart. It was the first time I imagined not being with them.

"I hope we'll all be together," Alice jumped in.

"Me too," echoed Layla, grabbing both of our hands. "Let's always be best friends, no matter what."

"Yes!" Alice and I exclaimed at the same time.

"Jinx!" we both yelled together.

"Double jinx!" We were both laughing hysterically.

"Seriously," Layla pleaded.

"Best friends no matter what," I repeated. Alice put an arm around each of us. And we hugged for a while. I really hope we stay together.

Before leaving, we built a sign that we put in front of the door. It said, *No Buddy is Home!*

It was late when I headed back to our camp. By the fire, Grandpa was finishing a story about the land claims agreement. I sat down and caught the end. "So our people worked very hard to arrive at this point when we will finally govern ourselves and become owners of our land. This is a huge moment in our history." I'm beginning to understand why everyone is so excited.

Just as Grandma, Grandpa, and I were walking to our tent, the northern lights came out! Magnificent swirling ghosts of green light pulsated through the sky, merging together and splitting apart. We stood watching for a while. I could watch them forever.

"The lights are dancing in the sky just like we will soon be dancing at the drum dance!" I said to Grandpa.

"Yes my girl, the *dagawo!*" he said and started singing, *"Hine'e he'e, he ho hine'e ha, hine'e he'e..."*

⸺෴⸺

I PUT away my journal and zip up my sleeping bag. I fall asleep hearing the drummers singing and seeing the northern lights dancing to the beat of the drums.

The Big Animal

WE'RE GETTING closer to the Assembly. Tomorrow, all the boats from the four communities will meet on an island near Behchokǫ̀. And the next day we'll all paddle to the community together!

Everyone is talking about self-government. And they're talking about land claims. "Thirty-nine thousand square kilometres of land will be Tłı̨chǫ land," I heard Grandma say.

I don't know how much land that is, but Auntie Rosaline says it's *ever lots*. I'm starting to get excited too. I try to imagine what that number looks like and how much space that would take. Thirty-nine plus three zeroes...

After leaving the campsite this morning, we paddled for many hours before finally reaching the portage. Our canoe was first to arrive. It was a tiny island covered in trees with a path that went straight across. We could see the other end of the trail.

That's when I saw him. The Big Animal. A towering black creature looking straight at us.

I was a little scared but mostly in awe. I wanted to say something, but I couldn't speak. It was *so big*. It looked ever powerful and kind of gentle at the same time. I've never been so close to the Big Animal before. I rubbed the branch in my pocket and kept looking at the beast.

Uncle Jimmy doesn't carry a gun, and he had no more bear bangers, which make super-loud noises like gunshots to scare the animal away. Instead he grabbed the kettle and started banging his paddle on it. It made ever lots of noise. He told us to stay calm and walk together. We walked in a line, following him on the trail while he whacked the kettle. As we walked straight towards the Big Animal, it moved through the forest in a 'U' shape around us. I followed Uncle Jimmy, watching the bear travel between the trees and over a massive rock. When we arrived at the end of the trail where we'd first seen the bear, it had reached our canoe and was sniffing our bags.

Uncle Jimmy made a fire by the water's edge. I caught my breath. "It's amazing that we share a planet with them, isn't it, Grandma?"

She explained to me how important it is to respect them. "Many years ago, there were two people who built a cabin near Wekweètì," she said. "They shot a bear and skinned it. Then they opened his mouth and used it as a quilt. They disrespected the spirit of the Big Animal. So

his spirit sent a curse on those people. There was nothing for them to eat that winter, and they froze."

I've heard it said many times that the spirit of the Big Animal is a very powerful one.

The other boats arrived at the start of the portage, and one of the crew bosses fired his gun into the sky. The Big Animal went away.

I spotted Alice and Layla and ran over to tell them what had happened.

"Were you scared?" Alice asked.

"It was kind of amazing," I replied. "Uncle Jimmy said it must have been looking for food."

"Well, it's a good thing it didn't try to eat *you!*" Layla exclaimed. We started laughing.

The mosquitoes were devouring me. They swarmed around my face and ears like a tornado, eating me alive. I grabbed the bug spray and put on ever lots. Alice and Kyle did the same. Auntie Rosaline told us we had to ration it or we might run out before reaching Behchokǫ̀.

"What does ration mean?" Kyle asked.

"Limit the amount of spray each person uses," Alice explained.

"I hate mosquitoes," he answered.

"Yeah, me too," I agreed. "Too bad we have to share the Earth with *them!*"

After we'd set off paddling again, I couldn't stop looking at the clouds. One side of the sky was like a priceless painting made up of many varying brushstrokes. The other side was like humungous cotton balls making all kinds of dreamy shapes. Lots of different birds were singing their songs. One of them had a lovely, elaborate melody. I kept trying to copy it until we were singing in unison. I forget how it goes now. I hope to hear it again tomorrow.

We passed a nest with many chicks, and the mama bird screeched at us until we were far ahead. It was

so cute how she protected her little ones. The water
sparkled like diamonds. The dragonflies were as big
as hummingbirds. We saw two beavers swimming
together across the lake. There was an abundance of
life everywhere.

The campground tonight is on rocky ground. It was
hard to find the right place to put the tent. Uncle Jimmy
found some good spots, but I wondered how we would
put the pegs through. He said that we wouldn't have to.
We'd put our bags or something heavy in each of the four
corners to hold the tent down.

After I finished helping, I went to find the others. We ran around the different camps. There were ever lots of wolves howling in the distance.

"Why are the wolves crying?" little Kyle asked.

"That's what wolves do," Layla answered with a warm smile. "They howl."

"I think it's because they want to play with us." Kyle said. "But they're not allowed to, so they're crying."

After supper, we went to sit next to Grandpa by the fire. I was happy he was talking about land claims and self-government. I want to learn all about it, even though it takes a lot of concentration.

"It took twelve years of negotiations to get here," he said. "Twelve years of trying to understand each

other. But we managed to combine land claims and self-government into one agreement, instead of two. Usually, they are two separate agreements. This is the first time in the Northwest Territories and only the second time in all of Canada that this has ever happened."

I don't fully understand what he was saying, but I do understand this agreement is *ever* important.

❧❦❧

I'M IN my tent. My mind is racing. I can't lie still. Tomorrow we'll be meeting all the other boats from the other communities!

I don't feel any pain tonight. I didn't feel any last night either. Maybe the branch is working after all.

Where the Water Does Not Freeze

WHAT A day! We were paddling across a very big lake when a huge storm hit us. Thunder and lightning and heavy rain fell on us. We were in the middle of the lake and far from shore. We all got soaking wet. The boat was filling up with water. Everyone paddled really hard to get to shore. Nobody spoke. I put my head down and stayed low, like I was taught to do before.

I squeezed what's left of my branch. It's more of a twig now. I prayed to the ancestor who had visited me in my dream. I understood what he meant about doing everything we can to be prepared but then needing to surrender to the Great Spirit. We were at the mercy of the weather. I prayed to the Great Spirit too, and to Uncle Joe. I prayed to everyone I could think of.

"Great Spirit, Creator, Uncle Joe, Tree, all the ancestors who have paddled these lakes, all of our ancestors," I prayed silently. "Please protect us from this storm. Please help us make it through. I will always listen to my Elders. I will be patient and know that everything has its time. Please keep us safe."

We finally made it to shore and waited under tarps for the storm to pass. Then we started a fire to warm up and have lunch.

While we were eating, Grandma told a story about the first time she heard a motor. Maybe she was thinking it would have been helpful to have a motor during that storm!

"Before, we had never heard motors," she said. "The first time people from Behchokǫ̀ came to Wekweètì with Ski-Doos and we heard them, we got really scared. We thought it was strangers coming to attack us, so we blew out all the candles in the tent. When they arrived, they asked us why we had no lights on." We all laughed.

A couple of the other Elders talked about electricity and running water coming to the community for the

first time. It was in the 1980s, not even that long ago!
Like twenty years. I'm amazed at how they lived without
these basic things that I always take for granted.

"Remember when we got phones?" Uncle Jimmy said
with a chuckle.

"How could I forget?" Grandma said. "Everybody
wanted one. They never thought that they were going
to get bills and things like that. So everybody hooked
up their phone in their houses and made ever lots of
calls. Next thing you know, one month later, the phone
bill came and they had all this money to pay." Everyone
laughed again.

"It's hard to believe that was less than twenty years ago," Auntie Rosaline said. "So much has changed so quickly. We even have Internet now."

After lunch, we set off again to meet on this island just outside Behchokǫ̀. As we were approaching the shore, Grandpa told the story of how their ancestors used to camp here.

"We call it 'net place island where the water does not freeze.' Near the island, a net can be set to catch fish where there will be open water throughout the winter," Grandpa explained. "The island has a long history of hosting our ancestors that came from the bush. They would renew kinship, tell stories, and celebrate. In later years, they would go to the trading post and use the island as a place to camp. It has a rich traditional fishing history. It is probably the place of our ancestors that we return to the most. There are still signs of the old tent rings."

In the afternoon, all the canoes from Whatì, Gamètì, and Behchokǫ̀ arrived. We sought out our friends from the other communities. Everyone hugged and laughed, happy to be reunited.

Our new village is gigantic. There are so many different camps. I heard there are sixty canoes altogether, with several hundred people and a couple hundred tents.

I helped set up our camp, and then I helped Grandma make bannock. It was ever delicious.

Hide and seek was the best! There were ever lots of people playing, and there were lots of places to hide. Kyle was following a cousin from Whatì, so I was spared him trailing after me.

Later, we hung out by the water. I motioned to Layla and Alice to follow me. I led them to a tree not far from the lake. We stood close together. "Thank you for the branch," I told them, and I showed them the little twig. "There isn't much left of it anymore. I feel better."

"So it helped you?" Layla asked.

"I think so," I answered. "I think Uncle Joe is a part of me, like all of our ancestors are. I think we are all a part of each other, all cultures, all people." Layla looked at

me with that intrigued expression on her face. "Even though this isn't my culture," I continued, "in a way it is. We all come from the same place. I think the same about the wind and the rain and the tree. Everything is connected. I want to leave what's left of this branch here where the water does not freeze. It can protect everyone who comes through."

"Good idea," Alice said.

"I'm so happy it helped." Layla nodded.

We hugged then huddled together. "Creator, Prophet, Uncle Joe, all of our ancestors, and all who guide us on this journey," I whispered. "*Mahsì* for your guidance. Please continue to watch over us and to guide us as we travel on these trails and through our lives." I laid the twig down by the tree. "We release this branch here, where the water never freezes, where the people always come. May it heal all who are in need." We put our heads down in silent prayer.

In the evening, everyone gathered in a huge circle and did a tea dance. We stood shoulder to shoulder, moving clockwise, and singing traditional songs. I was next to Grandpa. I could have danced all night. I don't want this trip to end.

Later, as we sat by the fire, Grandpa said the tea dance reminded him of last December, when he went to Ottawa.

"There were many stages our Agreement had to go through to come into effect once the negotiations were done," he said. "A bill is the name of something before it becomes law. For the Tłįchǫ Agreement to become law, the Tłįchǫ Bill had to pass. Passing the bill was the last stage the Agreement had to go through so that it could take effect."

I tried my best to follow everything, but it was hard. There were all these new words to keep track of—and words I thought I knew the meaning of, like "bill," which turned out to have a completely different meaning when talking about laws. Then he started adding dates. It was a lot of information.

"We went to Ottawa last December for the third reading of the Tłı̨chǫ Bill in the House of Commons. It takes three readings for a bill to pass. That means a bill needs to be presented three times before it becomes law. Then we went back again in February for the third reading in the Senate. It was very special. Many of us Tłı̨chǫ that were there had never left the North. We sat in the galleries watching Canada's democracy at work."

I know I'll need someone to explain it all again, but I still tried to understand as much as I could. I know democracy means that the people vote for their leaders. I know the House of Commons and the Senate have to do with the way the Canadian government works. But I don't really know what they are.

He went on. "After the Senate reading, we all stood in the Senate lobby, shoulder to shoulder in a circle, just like we did today. Everyone danced, and we sang our traditional songs. It was a very big tea dance in the lobby

of the Canadian Parliament. Government people were part of the circle. That is how we celebrated the final passage of the Tłı̨chǫ Bill."

I remember my mom telling me about that dance. She had gone to Ottawa with them, and I had slept at Layla's house. I really wish I'd been there too!

"Tomorrow we will paddle to Behchokǫ̀," Grandpa continued with his arm in the air and hand pointing towards the community, while Grandma cooked bannock over the fire. "There, we will celebrate the day we officially have our own self-government and become owners of our land."

That's when it hit me. That's when I realized what an important moment in history this is.

DAY 10

~~~~~~~~

Behchokǫ̀

WE ARRIVED in Behchokǫ̀ this morning! I could hardly sit still. Guns fired as we approached the land. Thousands of people were lined up to meet us on the shore. The line went up the hill and through the community as far as I could see.

The closer we got to land, the more excited I was. I couldn't stop laughing. As soon as we beached our canoes, I spotted my mom in the crowd and ran over to her. We hugged for a long time. I didn't want to let her go.

Then we began shaking hands with everyone waiting on land. It's a tradition at the end of a trip that all travellers shake hands with every person waiting to greet them and say *Mahsì,* or "thank you." Once in a while someone, usually an Elder, would hold my hand a little longer, a little more tightly, and say *Mahsì cho,* or "thank you very much." It felt ever good. It went on for a long time. I must have shaken over a thousand hands today!

When the greetings were over, I carried my bag up to my mom's friend's house where we're staying. There are about twenty people sleeping here this week. I talked nonstop about the trip. There was so much I wanted to tell Mom: the story of the Prophet's Grave and the branch, my dream of the ancestor, getting lost on my way back from the waterfall, the abandoned prospector's cabin, learning how to paddle with such speed, getting over my fear of the Big Animal...

"Wow!" said Mom. "Sounds like a very eventful trip! Did you have time to write in your journal?"

"Every day! I drew a lot too," I said proudly. "Thanks, Mom, for everything."

"I'm so happy you enjoyed it, sweetie." She smiled at me and stroked my hair.

"I *loved* it!" I exclaimed. "Can I go back next year?"

"Of course," she answered. "Maybe we can go together."

She looked at me for a moment without saying anything. I could see so much love in her eyes. "You have grown remarkably in the last ten days, Jules. I can tell this journey has been a rite of passage for you. I'm sure Uncle Joe would be very proud of you."

"I miss him a lot, Mom."

"Me too." She hugged me and held me for a while. I was crying. I didn't pull away this time. It felt good to cry in my mama's arms.

I took a shower for the first time in ten days. It felt ever good. I couldn't believe how much I missed hot water. After I got dressed, Mom told me she was going to the community hall for the final Dogrib Treaty 11 Council annual gathering ever.

"Why is it the last one ever?" I asked, confused.

"This is the last Assembly of the *Council*," she explained. "Tomorrow is the effective date of the Tłįchǫ Agreement, so it will be the first day of the Tłįchǫ Assembly and the first annual gathering of the *Tłįchǫ Government*."

"What exactly does effective date mean?" I asked.

"It means the day the Tłı̨chǫ Agreement comes into being."

I still don't know exactly what everything means, but I do know *this is huge!* And it's so exciting to be a part of it. I asked Mom what they were going to do at the meeting. "Regular business," she replied. "Reviewing financial statements and awarding scholarships to Tłı̨chǫ students."

In the evening, we gathered for a wedding, feast, and dagawo, or drum dance. When someone gets married in the communities, everybody goes. Long tables filled the cultural centre. Every seat was taken. I sat at a table with my mom, Layla, and her family. Many of the men wore their traditional beaded vests, and many of the older women were dressed in blue and purple with scarves tied around their necks. The foreman went to each table serving everyone, as is the tradition in their feasts. We ate caribou, bannock, rice pudding, hot dogs, apples, and cookies. So yummy. Then the countdown to midnight . . . the countdown to the effective date!

At midnight there were dazzling fireworks.

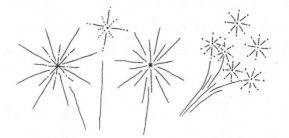

"Wow! Look at that!" Alice said.

"Ever cool!" I was fascinated. I had never seen fireworks before, except on TV. Most people there had never seen them in real life either.

"So many colours," Layla added, "and shapes."

"E-v-e-r." Alice dragged out the word a long time.

I heard a few Elders beside us saying they weren't happy that the noise of the fireworks sounded like war, not like celebration. "This noise is not good for the fish," one Elder said, shaking his head. I guess it might scare them.

The drum dance followed after the fireworks, and the evening ended with an ever-huge tea dance. I could hear the echoes of the ancestors singing.

There's so much more I want to write, but I'm too tired. I have to go to sleep. Tomorrow is the big day!

DAY 11

The Effective Date

WHEN I WOKE UP this morning, everyone in the house was already having breakfast. Mom made all my favourites—scrambled eggs with cheese, caribou ribs, bacon, hash browns, and pancakes. And there was ever lots of fresh fruit.

Mom told me about the effective date. "Two years ago, the prime minister of Canada, the premier of the Northwest Territories, the Grand Chief, and four community Chiefs signed the Tłįchǫ Agreement. Today, it becomes a reality."

After breakfast, all the adults went to the community hall, where the meetings were taking place. I went

with them. I wanted to see how the Agreement would become effective.

The drummers walked into the room dressed in their beaded hide vests. I love the smell of freshly tanned hide. Behind them followed the members of the Tłı̨chǫ Assembly. Grandpa told me, "There is the Grand Chief, the four Tłı̨chǫ community government Chiefs, two councillors from each community, and the speaker."

He turned to look at me. "The 14th Dogrib Treaty 11 annual gathering is over. The first Tłı̨chǫ annual gathering now begins." I couldn't stop fidgeting. I wanted to sing and dance, I was so excited.

The bishop and drummers led the opening prayer. Then the priest swore in the Tłı̨chǫ Assembly members. After that, they passed the first Tłı̨chǫ laws, and the Grand Chief and other Assembly members made speeches. Grandpa repeated, "This is the first Tłı̨chǫ annual gathering and the first sitting of the Tłı̨chǫ Assembly."

When the speeches were over, we went outside and gathered in front of the community hall for the flag-raising ceremony. A group of children sang "O Canada" in Tłı̨chǫ. It was so beautiful. I wished I knew it and could sing with them. People laughed and cheered.

I saw Grandma crying and ran up to her. "What's wrong?" I asked.

"We have waited so long for this, my girl," she answered. "I can't believe I am seeing it in my lifetime. It is a huge moment in our history." Her tears were joyful, not sad.

A Tłı̨chǫ Elder took down the old Dogrib Treaty 11 Council flag. And the new Tłı̨chǫ Government flag was presented. Everyone cheered.

The new flag was raised. A man started explaining the symbols on the flag. "He was one of the negotiators for the Tłı̨chǫ Agreement, and he designed the new flag," Mom told me.

"The royal blue background represents the Tłı̨chǫ Nation territory," the man said. "The four tipis represent

the four Tłı̨chǫ communities, which together form the Tłı̨chǫ Nation, Government, and Assembly. The sun and river represent the words of the great Chief Monfwi, who signed Treaty 11 in 1921. As long as the sun rises and sets and the river flows forward and not backward, the Tłı̨chǫ People will honour the Treaty. Finally, the North Star represents direction and a new era for the Tłı̨chǫ Nation, which moves united into the future."

"What a cool flag!" I told my mom. "It has so much meaning."

Afterwards, there were some flag and gift presentations and more speeches. Mom said the people giving speeches had helped get the Tłı̨chǫ Bill passed.

One of the speakers said something I keep thinking about: "The Tłı̨chǫ have always been self-governing. Today is really a symbol of the government's recognition of these rights." The drummers made a prayer to close the ceremony.

In the early evening, we went to the cultural centre for another delicious feast. There was ever lots of dry fish that people brought from Whatı̀. More gifts were given. More speeches were made. Then we had the best drum dance ever!

All the tables were cleared. First the drummers began hitting their drums slowly and solemnly, singing the opening prayer and making the cultural centre a sacred space. Everyone stood around, bowing their heads. I did too, and closed my eyes. When the prayer was over, everyone did the sign of the cross three times.

Then the drummers started drumming and singing with so much power and passion. Layla, Alice, and I danced and danced and danced. We took turns following each other into the circle. When we would get to the side of the circle where the drummers were, I would close my eyes for a moment and feel the drum beating in my chest.

There were so many people dancing that sometimes there were four or five circles around each other. Little kids were bouncing around, and many Elders were dancing too, some with their canes. There was a live band nearby and some two-step and jigging, but we didn't go anywhere else. Grandpa, Grandma, Uncle Jimmy, Uncle Gordie, Auntie Rosaline, Mom, little Kyle, and hundreds of other people were dancing with us. We spent the whole night at the dagawo. My cheeks still hurt from all the smiling and laughter. I'm sure the ancestors were dancing too.

Flying Home

I WAS so busy the last few nights, I had no time to write. Drum dances, feasts, hand games, and all kinds of other celebrations continued throughout the weekend. It was ever fun.

The morning after the effective date, we all gathered to feed the fire. It's a ceremony to give thanks, to pray to the Creator and those who have passed away. Food and tobacco offerings are thrown into the fire, and many prayers are made.

I had a piece of Grandma's bannock and some cookies. I offered them to the fire and whispered, "Mahsì." I was talking to the Creator, to Uncle Joe, to all the

ancestors, and to the one who visited me that night. I was talking to everyone who has come before me.

After the ceremony, the adults went back to the meeting room for nominations of the Grand Chief. When I grow up I'd like to be a leader like him. I'd like to help protect the land and rights for all people.

Now I'm on the plane, flying back to Wekweètì. I look down at the land and trails of the ancestors, and I feel so grateful to be part of it all.

I'm grateful to the Tłı̨chǫ People for adopting me into their world and taking me on this journey. I'm grateful to my mother and all of my ancestors for who I am today. And I'm grateful to the land for all of its gifts. What a trip!

Author's Note

THIS BOOK is inspired by the people of Wekweètì, who took me in over twenty years ago and became like a second family to me. I went out on the land and partook in countless ceremonies and dances with them.

More particularly, the book is inspired by the youth who were on the annual canoe trip in 2013, when we travelled from Wekweètì to Behchokǫ̀.

The old-time stories told by Grandpa and Grandma are true stories that were shared with me by Elders of Wekweètì, especially Alexis Arrowmaker, Mary Adele Tsatchia, and Louis Whane. I recorded them, with their permission, between 2002 and 2005. I also included a couple of stories by Joseph and Madeline Judas.

I first met the Tłįchǫ when I moved to Wekweètì in 1999 to work as the Dechi Laot'i First Nations band manager. Dechi Laot'i means "people from the edge of the treeline." We were about 130 people. I lived there for a few years in my house by the edge of Snare Lake.

Managing the community was an incredible learning experience and an opportunity to make a difference in people's lives. But what inspired me most were the people, their culture, their rituals, and the land. I got to know all of them well. I went out on the land whenever I could with people from the community. Weekends were filled with hunting, fishing, boat rides, visits, and picnics at the beach or cemetery. Kids often came over to my house to play and colour. My time in the community has greatly altered my view of the world and perception of life.

I arrived in Wekweètì at a time when negotiations for the Tłįchǫ Agreement were underway. In 1992, the Dogrib Treaty 11 Council was mandated to negotiate a Dogrib Nation Regional comprehensive Claim, which later became known as the Tłįchǫ Agreement. I became part of what was happening in the four communities. And when I left Wekweètì from late 2002 until the effective date, I was part of the team to prepare for the eventual government.

Every summer, people were travelling to the annual gathering by canoe, retracing different trails of their ancestors. There were youth, Elders, and invited people on these trips. I always wanted to go, but I couldn't because I was part of the workforce.

In 2003, I had the privilege of being in Behchokǫ̀ when the Agreement was signed by Prime Minister Jean Chrétien, Premier Stephen Kakfwi of the Northwest Territories, Grand Chief Joe Rabesca, and the Chiefs of the four communities. To open the celebrations Elder Alexis Arrowmaker and the Grand Chief each took an arm of the prime minister and led him in a historic Tea Dance. Photos of this moment appeared in newspapers around the world. I was also in Ottawa with the Tłı̨chǫ during the third reading of their Bill and the momentous Tea Dance in the Senate Lobby.

In 2005, I watched the canoes arrive in Behchokǫ̀ for the annual gathering and effective date of the Tłı̨chǫ Agreement. I wrote an article about that week, which appeared in *News North*. I then began a professional artistic career as a singer-songwriter and spoken-word artist. Years later, former Chief Negotiator John B. Zoe planted the seed for what was to become this book. He suggested I write a children's story based on that article to teach the youth about this important time in history.

In 2012, I had the chance to take part in my first Tłı̨chǫ canoe trip retracing the trails of their ancestors, which went from Behchokǫ̀ to Wekweètì. Paddling into the community where I had lived for several years was like a dream to me. The canoe trip is not only an opportunity to retrace the ancestors' trails, it's also a way of transferring energy to the community members. The travellers coming by canoe harness the power of the land, and those energies are then passed on to the rest of the people at the annual gathering.

The following summer, I returned again for a canoe trip from Wekweètì to Behchokǫ̀. This time I travelled with the people from Wekweètì. I had a chance to observe the community on the journey, especially the young people. I watched their excitement being on the trails with their Elders, growing and learning. I watched the young ones who were taking the trip for the first time and tried to see it all through their eyes.

I feel this book is important on many levels. First for the Tłı̨chǫ youth, as it was originally intended to have more written resources of their significant history. Also for my son and all youth, to know a little more about these Indigenous stories upon which our country was founded. And finally, I think it's important for stories to have more strong female lead characters to empower young girls.

I feel honoured to have been trusted with these stories and given the blessing to bring them forth. I hope I have done well by them.

For more information about the Tłįchǫ People, visit tlicho.ca.

Acknowledgements

I DON'T think anything would be possible without the love and support of family and friends. To that end, it's impossible for me to name every person that has helped in the making of this book. But I am extremely grateful to all of you.

To all the Elders of Wekweètì who shared their stories with me and showed me their old-time way of life. Especially Alexis and Elizabeth Arrowmaker, Madeline Judas Sr., Joe and Rosa Pea'a, Mary Adele Eyakfwo, Joe Boline, and Louis and Elizabeth Whane. Masì.

To Joseph and Madeline Judas, masì for all your stories and for taking me to your cabin at the end of the lake to experience living off the land for an extended period. I learned so much from you.

To the youth on the 2012 canoe trip who inspired this story. Masì cho. Especially Laylu, Keaira, Mackenzie, Tylene, Belinda, Victoria, Jimmy Joe, Rachel, Nikki, and Thiona.

To every member of Wekweètì, thank you for taking me in over twenty years ago and teaching me your ways. My time living with you helped shape my vision of life and who I am today. Especially Johnny Arrowmaker, who took me on countless fishing and hunting trips, Cece Judas and Clarence Nasken, who always give me a home when I return, Georgie Kodzin and Patti Magrum, who took me in their camp, and Adeline Football, for all your assistance in this project and for always bringing me back. So many others here that should be named but aren't. Masì. You've each touched my life in some way.

To John B. Zoe. Thank you for everything. You are an inspiration. Most importantly, masì for planting the seed of this book and helping me nourish it to life.

To Tammy Steinwand, for coming though in so many ways. I couldn't have done this without you. Masì. And to Archie Beaverho for the beautiful illustrations and wonderful collaboration. I look forward to more of them.

Mahsì, Antoine Mountain, for your ongoing encouragement and support and for helping me to find a home for this book. I am extremely grateful.

Thank you to Heritage House Publishing. Especially Lara Kordic for believing in my vision and helping it come to life. Thanks also to Sarah Harvey for your insight, to Setareh Ashrafologhalai for the beautiful layout and design, and to Leslie Kenny and Nandini Thaker for all your work behind the scenes.

Thank you Mary Metcalfe for all the work and enthusiasm you put into this project. Masì also to Terrell Knapton-Pain for providing us with the map.

To Barbara and Carrie. Thank you for reading an early draft and giving me invaluable feedback that helped shape the story. To Rayne, thanks for your insight. And to my original writing group, especially Christina, Louise, and Charlotte for helping me develop my vision when it was still just an idea in my mind. Also thanks to Pierre, Laura, Eleni, and Neal for your feedback.

To the Conseil des arts et des lettres du Quebec, merci for taking a chance with this story and to the Tłı̨chǫ Government for your ongoing support. Masì.

Finally to my dad, Jean, who passed away before this was done; to my dearest mom, Mimi; and extraordinary brother, Alain. Thank you for always being there for me.

The following pages contain a few photos from my canoe trips with the Tłı̨chǫ.

NADINE NEEMA is a graduate of McGill University's Faculty of Management. She first began working with the Tłįchǫ in 1999, as the community manager of Wekweètì, a small isolated Tłįchǫ com-  munity in the Northwest Territories, then assisting with their land claims and self-government negotiations under Chief Negotiator John B. Zoe. Since the landmark Tłįchǫ Agreement in 2005, Neema has maintained a strong bond with the community and returns periodically to conduct youth workshops and other activities. With her long international experience in music and song writing, being mentored by Leon- ard Cohen and opening for artists such as Joe Cocker and Cyndi Lauper, Neema has written a song with the community youth entitled "Oh Wekweètì" and pro- duced a Christmas concert at the school. She has also photographed many community events and produced photography books for them. Born in Montreal of Egyptian and Lebanese descent, Nadine lives between Montreal and St-Adolphe-d'Howard with her son. Over the last five years, she has developed a passion for gardening and growing their own food. For more infor- mation, visit neema.ca.

ARCHIE BEAVERHO is an accomplished painter and illustrator, whose Tłı̨chǫ Dene culture is reflected in his work. He creates paintings of spiritual activities of his people, like drum dancing, hand games, and hunting. He paints stories of  how people used to live on the land and used medicine for guidance and healing.

When he was a little boy he lived with his grandparents. One day his grandfather gave him a white sheet of paper and coloured pencils and told him to do a drawing of his friends, who were playing outside. His grandfather told him that he would one day make a name for himself through his art. When he was in school, he drew the plane that used to come to the community to bring school supplies. When the pilot saw it, he offered to take Archie and his classmates on a plane ride as a trade for the drawing.

When Archie was about thirteen, he started working with clay. He grabbed some clay from a lake, put it on a board, and started playing with it, just to feel it and move it. He made a bird out of the clay. Today he uses soapstone to carve animals. He lives in Behchokǫ̀ with his common-law partner and their two boys. Their daughter lives nearby.